Harry hates his sister Maggie. She's always messing up his stuff—rearranging the trees around his electric trains or feeding hamburger to his Venus's-flytrap (which promptly drops dead). When she's not sneaking around behind his back, Maggie's pestering Harry for help with her homework or stealing the rose off his birthday cake. Yet, despite all this, no one believes he hates her. But he does.

She's only a little girl, his parents tell him. She doesn't know any better. Harry ought, they say, to set an example for her. But if Harry wants to set anything for Maggie, it's a trap—preferably one with snarling tigers and creepy extraterrestrials, who might remove her to another planet.

Only when Harry is let in on a family secret does he start to consider, reluctantly, that sometimes hate may be mixed in with love.

In *I Hate My Sister Maggie*, a sequel to her popular *I Hate My Brother Harry*, Crescent Dragonwagon writes with wit and empathy. Her feisty, true-to-life text will amuse and reassure every young reader who has ever hated a sibling. Humorous pictures by Leslie Morrill underscore the text perfectly. *I Hate My Sister Maggie* is a book children will read over and over.

I Hate
My Sister Maggie

Crescent Dragonwagon

illustrated by Leslie Morrill

Macmillan Publishing Company   New York

...but I <u>love</u> my editor Judith
—C.D.

To Arthur and Leona Morrill
—L.M.

Text copyright © 1989 by Crescent Dragonwagon
Illustrations copyright © 1989 by Leslie Morrill
Macmillan Publishing Company
866 Third Avenue, New York, NY 10022
Collier Macmillan Canada, Inc.
First Edition   Printed in the United States of America

10 9 8 7 6 5 4 3 2 1

The text of this book is set in 14 point Kennerly.
The illustrations are rendered in pencil and watercolor.

Library of Congress Cataloging-in-Publication Data
Dragonwagon, Crescent.
I hate my sister Maggie / by Crescent Dragonwagon;
illustrated by Leslie Morrill.   p.   cm.
Summary: Harry is fed up with his brat of a younger sister,
until his mother tells him a secret that puts things in
a totally different perspective.
ISBN 0-02-733150-4
[1. Brothers and sisters—Fiction.] I. Morrill, Leslie H., ill.
II. Title. PZ7.D7824Iae 1989 [E]—dc19 88-8197 CIP AC

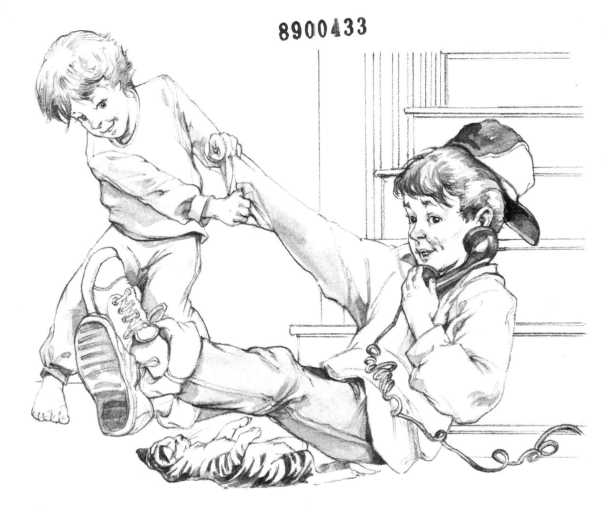

I hate my sister Maggie.

When my aunt Jane calls, she always asks me,

"How is Maggie?"

"Okay," I say.

"You don't sound very enthusiastic," says my aunt Jane.

"I'm not," I say. "I hate her."

"You do *not* hate your sister," says Aunt Jane.

But I do. No one believes me.

"I'm surprised at you," says my aunt. "A big boy like you is supposed to set an example for his sister." I don't tell her, but I would rather set a trap, than be an example, for Maggie. I could bait it with Clark bars, and there'd be hidden tigers. Maggie'd trip

reaching for the Clark bars, and the tigers would get her. "Help, help, Harry!" she'd yell, but I wouldn't help her. "They're going to eat me up!"

"Serves you right," I'd say, and walk away.

"Bon appétit, tigers."

*T*hat's what my father said to us last week, when he took us to Algeo's for sundaes. "Bon appétit, kids."

"What's 'bon appétit' mean?" Maggie asked me.

"'Good appetite,'" I told her. "It's French."

"That's stupid," said Maggie, "and I don't believe you."

"Don't believe me then," I said. "And you're the one who's stupid."

"Chil·dren," said my father, "don't make me sorry I brought you to Algeo's."

"She started it!" I said. "You heard her!"

"Yes, I heard her," said my father. "And, Maggie, it was wrong to call your brother stupid. But, Harry, you're old enough to know better than to answer back the same way. Maggie, your brother is right. 'Bon appétit' does mean 'good appetite' or 'enjoy your food.'"

"I did enjoy my food," said Maggie, "but now it's all gone." She looked at her empty sundae dish, and then she looked at mine. All I'd eaten was the cherry from the top and one perfect bite with a little of the ice cream, the whipped cream, the chocolate, and some nuts. I like to eat a sundae slowly, with some of everything in each bite. "Yes," said Maggie, "mine's all gone, all, all gone. Harry, can I have a bite of yours?" "No! Dad, tell her!" I said.

"Maggie, let your brother eat his sundae in peace," my father said. "You already had yours."

Then he said, "I'm going to get a paper,"
and he left me with that brat of a sister.
"Please, Harry, please please please can I have a bite?"
"No."
"But you have all that, and I don't have any."
"You already had yours."
"Oh, come on, just one bite, please please please?"
"No."
"You're mean! I think you're mean mean mean!
Just one bite!"

I put down my spoon. "Maggie, will you quit?"

"Mean! I hate you, Harry!"

"Well, I hate you, so we're even."

"Why won't you give me just one bite?"

"You're such a pig, Maggie! First you gobble up yours in
two seconds like a big fat pig, and then you want to eat
mine. Pig!"

Then my stupid sister started yelling so loudly that
everyone in Algeo's turned around. "DADDYYYYYY!
Harry called me a pig!"

My father came running over with the paper. "No
sundaes for either of you next week. And just for that,
young man, you can sit in the backseat on the way home."

"I hate Maggie."

"Oh, no, you don't," says my father. "How can you hate
your sister?"

But I do.

When I had my electric trains set up in my room, Maggie came in when I wasn't there and moved all the trees to different places. I told my mother, and she said, "But can't you just move the trees back to where they were, Harry?"

"Well, sure, but they're *my* trains and she shouldn't have moved them! She shouldn't have been in my room in the first place!"

"You're right, Harry," said my mother. "She shouldn't have. But she's only a little girl. And, honey, you're four years older than she is. You're practically grown-up compared to her."

But when I was as old as she is now, it was the same story. "She's only a baby, Harry," they told me then. "She's only a toddler." I used to play with Tinkertoys then, and I remember once I worked two days building this giant castle and she came in and knocked it down. "She's only a toddler, Harry. She didn't know she was ruining your castle—she just liked the sound of its falling." Ha! I'd like to hear the sound of *her* falling—like from Mars into outer space. One loud "You're MEEEEEEEAN, HARRY!" and then she'd be gone forever, lost in the galaxies.

I should have dropped her in a black hole in space years
ago. Then I could have *always* had the rose on my
birthday cake. This year I finally got it again, but for the
last three years it was, "There's only one rose, Harry.
Why don't you be nice and give it to your sister? After
all, look at all your presents—can't you be generous and
give her the rose? She doesn't understand it's your
birthday—all she sees is that you're getting everything
and she isn't. Look, you can have the leaves."

But I didn't want the leaves. I wanted the rose.
It was *my* birthday cake. I should have had it.
But she always gets her way.
I hate her.
"Oh, Harry, you get annoyed with Maggie sometimes, but
you don't hate her," says my father.
I do too hate her.

The other day I was trying to do my homework at the kitchen table. Maggie was doing hers, which means trying to get me to do it for her.

"What's two and four, Harry?"

"You figure it out."

"I can't!"

"Yes, you can. Now leave me alone. I'm trying to work."

"But you know what it is! Come on, Harry. Just tell me, please please please? Just what's two and four?"

To shut her up, I said, "Okay, it's six. Now would you please bug off?"

Just then my mother walked in. "Harry! You shouldn't give her the answers like that. How will she learn? And don't tell your sister to bug off."

Maggie is always getting me in trouble. I hate her.

If I had one sister, and I sold her to an extraterrestrial, how many sisters would I have?

None. I'd like that a lot.

I can still remember when they brought her home from the hospital. She was really ugly, wrinkled up like a prune and bright red. I kind of liked her though, then. When I put my hand in her crib, she'd grab one of my fingers and squeeze it, hard. I remember I was surprised at how strong she was for being so little. Back then, we *both* used to ride in the front seat. She'd be in her little car seat and I'd sit next to her and show her things. "Sky, Maggie," I'd say. "Truck. Store. Tree." She was too little to understand, but she seemed to look where I pointed. She always had this funny, surprised expression on her face. Sometimes I'd laugh at her, and she'd smile.

I was the first one she ever smiled at, and the first word
she said was "Har," then "Kitty," then "Ma," then
"Da." I was proud that she said my name first, but my
father said, "Well, I don't mind your mother and me
coming after you, Harry, but after the *cat*?" How could
I know that that little prune would turn into a brat
who got the rose off my birthday cake for three straight
years and who still, almost always, gets the front seat
to herself?

And how could I know she'd feed hamburger to my Venus's-fly-trap and kill it? I grew it on my windowsill for two months for Science Fair last year, and she murdered it by feeding it hamburger, and I had to do some dumb experiment with molds instead, and I only got third prize. I know I would have gotten first with a Venus's-fly-trap. Plus I had to throw out the sign on carnivorous plants I'd spent three days making.

"Well, I didn't know it was going to die!" Maggie said. "I was just trying to help you feed the stupid plant!"

"Help it! You *murdered* it!"

"Harry," said my father, "she said she was sorry. She's told you she was trying to help."

"Some help! What was she doing in my room anyway? Why do you let her get away with messing up every single thing I do?"

"But, Harry, she's little. She didn't know any better."

"She should have asked me. She should be fed to a giant Venus's-fly-trap. I hate her!"

"Oh, Harry, you don't mean that."

I do too mean it. If I ever find a giant Venus's-fly-trap, I'll prove it.

My mother always says, "Well, what about when she got turned around in her crib with her head under the covers and you called me because you were afraid she'd suffocate?" My mother always brings that up.
She said it again today.
"I didn't know she'd turn out to be a brat," I told my mother. "If I had, I wouldn't have called you."
"What about when she had appendicitis and was in the hospital and you said, 'Gee, it sure is quiet here without Maggie'?"
"It *was* quiet, Mom! I liked it quiet. I wish it was quiet all the time!"

"Then why did you tell me you missed her then?
  You know you did."
"Okay, I missed her when she was in the hospital—big
  deal. Maybe I like her when she's gone. But when she's
  here I hate her."
"Always?" asked my mom.
"Most of the time. Sometimes she's okay, but I usually
  hate her."
"If she's okay sometimes, you don't hate her,"
  said my mother.
"You just get angry with her, like all brothers and sisters
  do. Anyway ... " She stops for a second. "Come into the
  kitchen, Harry. I want to tell you a secret."

We went into the kitchen. Through the window I could
see Maggie and my dad watering the lawn outside.
"You want the last piece of lemon meringue pie?" my
mother asked me.
"Do I have to split it with Maggie?"
"Nope," said my mother. "Whole thing. Special treat." She
put it down on a plate and got me a glass of milk too.

"What's the secret?" I asked her.

"I think," she said, "that you may finally have the ultimate revenge on Maggie."

"Revenge?" I said. "What do you mean?"

I forked off a piece of pie.

My mother said, "Well, I'm going to have another baby."

"WHAT?" I put down my fork. "You're *what?*
Are you kidding?"

"Nope," said my mother. "In November you're going to
have another little sister or a brother."

"Oh, no!" I said. "How can you call it revenge? One is
already too many!"

"Ah," said my mother. "But, Harry, think. You'll still be
the oldest, but Maggie will no longer be the youngest.
We'll say to her, 'Maggie, be nice to the baby. He's
littler than you.' Or, 'Maggie, you have to set an example
for your sister.'"

I thought about it. "You mean," I said, "the baby will get to ride in the front seat?"

"That's right."

"And the baby will wreck Maggie's stuff?"

"I'm afraid so."

"And kill her Venus's-fly-trap?"

"Maybe, if she ever grows one."

"And the baby will get the rose on her birthday cake?"

"Well," said my mother, "I've been thinking we should just get bigger cakes with more roses. I can't take another who-gets-the-rose fight."

"Cakes with three roses?"

"Three roses."

I picked up my fork and ate the bite of lemon meringue pie I had cut. Then I ate another bite and had some milk. It tasted very good.

"Well," I said, "it might get better, but it might get worse, you know."

"True," said my mother.

I had another bite of pie. "Do you think it will be a boy or a girl?" I asked her.

"I don't know," she said.

"Do you think it will look as ugly as Maggie did when she first came home from the hospital?"

"Probably," said my mother. "You looked pretty ugly too—although I thought you were the handsomest baby ever born."

I looked out the window again, at Maggie and my father in the backyard.

"You haven't told Maggie yet?" I asked my mother.

"Nope," my mother said.

"Why not?" I asked her.

"Because," she said, "I thought you should know first. After all, you're the oldest."

I ate my pie, wondering if it would be better or worse. Maybe when the baby gets big, I thought, we can gang up on Maggie. On the other hand, what if the baby and Maggie gang up on me?

I wondered if this baby's first word would be 'Har' too. It had better not be 'Mag.' I thought about how even Maggie was okay when she was a little pruney-looking baby, although she grew up into a brat. I thought about how maybe this baby would be okay too and *maybe* not grow up into a brat.

But what if this baby is a *worse* brat?

I finished my pie.

"Can I be the one to tell Maggie?" I asked my mother.

"I thought you hated Maggie," she said.

"I do," I told her. "But sometimes she's okay."